祖母的星期六汤

Grandma's Saturday Soup

Written by Sally Fraser

Illustrated by Derek Brazell

Mandarin translation by Sylvia Denham

星期一早上，妈妈很早便叫醒我。
「咪咪，起床，穿衣服上学。」
我睡眼疲困的爬下床，将窗帘拉开。

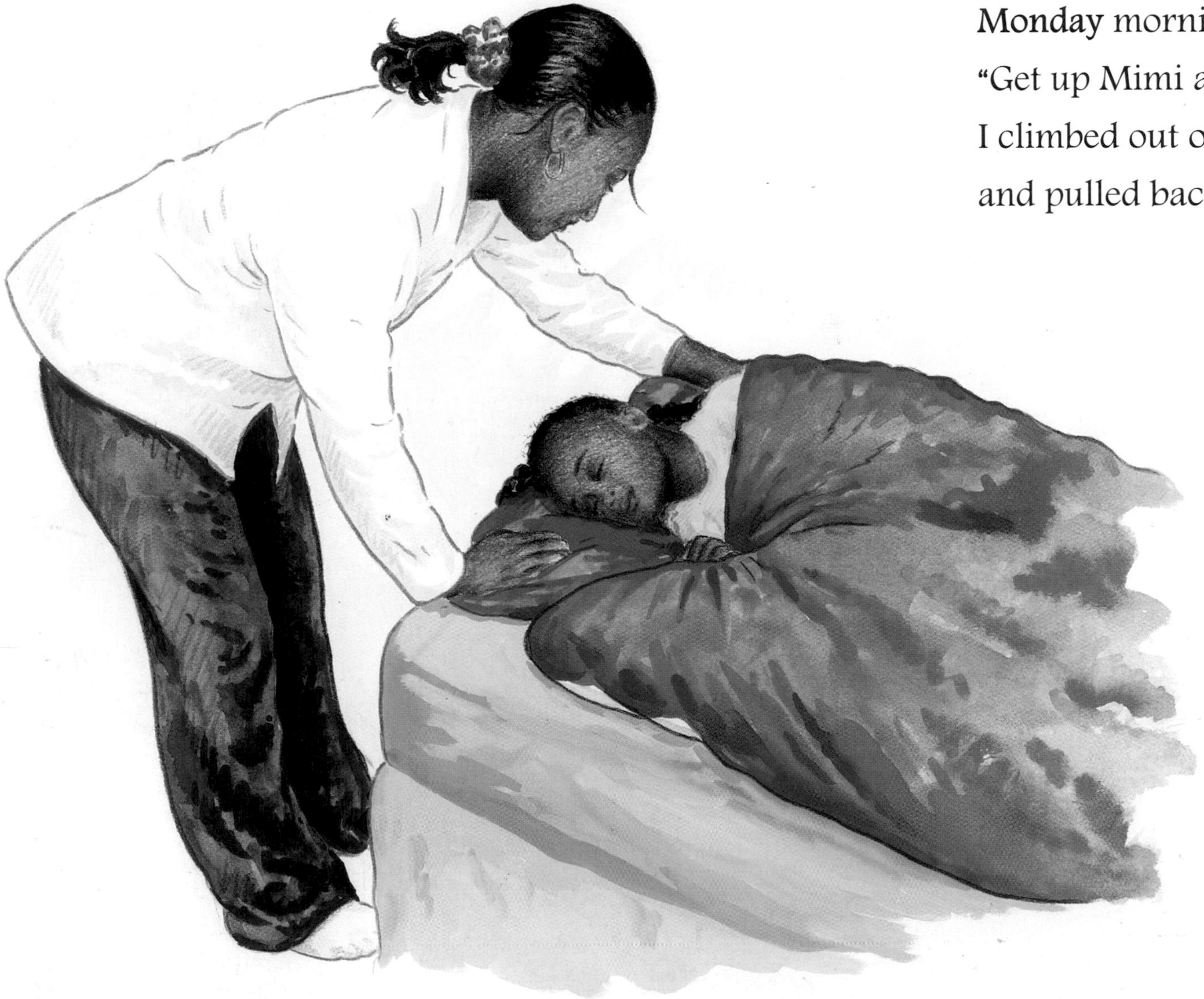

Monday morning Mum woke me early.
"Get up Mimi and get dressed for school."
I climbed out of bed all sleepy and tired,
and pulled back the curtains.

早上密云和寒冷，
天上的云是白色和松软的，
它们令我想起祖母的星期六汤的汤团。

The morning was cloudy and cold.
The clouds in the sky were white and fluffy.
They reminded me of the dumplings in Grandma's Saturday Soup.

当我去祖母的家时，她讲有关牙买加的故事给我听。

Grandma tells me stories about Jamaica when I go to her house.

「牙买加的云会带来豪雨，
好像有人在天空开了水喉一样，
温和的清风将它们吹送，太阳又再次出来了。」

"The clouds in Jamaica bring the heaviest rain.
It's like someone has turned the tap on in the sky.
The warm breeze moves them on and the sun comes out again."

星期二早上，爸爸带我上学。
这天很寒冷和清新，昨晚曾下过雪。

Tuesday morning Dad took me to school.
The day was cold and crisp; it had snowed in the night.

它是白色和柔滑的，很似切开了的甘薯里面一样，
就好像祖母的星期六汤的甘薯。

It’s white and smooth and looked like the inside of a sliced yam.
Just like the yam in Grandma's Saturday Soup.

祖母告诉我沙滩上的细沙好像新雪一样，
但却不会寒冷。

Grandma tells me that the white powdery sand on the beaches looks like fresh snow but it's never cold.

我能否用白沙造一个沙人呢？
那一定很有趣?!

I wonder if I could make a sandman with the white sand?
Wouldn't that be funny?!

星期三的雪下得更大，非常寒冷，
但我穿得很温暖。
当我去祖母的家时，
她讲有关牙买加的故事给我听。

Wednesday the snow fell harder. It was cold but I was wrapped up warm.

Grandma tells me stories about Jamaica when I go to her house.

「太阳每天照耀，令肌肤温暖，
你只需要穿短裤和 T-恤。」
每天都和暖？短裤和 T-恤？
我真不能相信。

"The sun shines every day. The sun is warm on your skin
and you only need to wear your shorts and a T-shirt."
Warm every day? Shorts and T-shirt? I can't believe that.

下午休息时，我们造雪球，互相抛掷。

At afternoon play we made snowballs
and threw them at each other.

The snowballs remind me of the round soft potatoes in Grandma's Saturday Soup.

那些雪球令我想起祖母的星期六汤的马铃薯。

星期四放学后，我和我的朋友莉娜跟她的妈妈去图书馆。

On **Thursday** I went to the library after school with my friend Layla and her Mum.

我们路过公园时，看到两个小球茎开始发芽，
嫩绿的苗芽在雪中凸出。
它们就好像祖母的星期六汤的青葱。

As we passed the park we saw the little bulbs starting to grow.
The little green shoots poked through the snow. They looked like
the spring onions in Grandma's Saturday Soup.

Grandma tells me about the wonderful plants and flowers in Jamaica.
"In Jamaica the most beautiful flowers grow wild.
They are all different colours and sizes
and their smell fills the air."
I've never seen flowers like that before,
I wonder if she's only joking?

祖母告诉我有关牙买加的奇妙植物和花卉。
「在牙买加，最漂亮的花是野生的，
它们有各种不同的颜色和大小，
空气更充满著它们的清香。」
我从来未见过这样的花，她是否在开玩笑呢？

星期五，爸爸和妈妈迟了上班。
「快，咪咪，挑一个水果，带到学校去。」

On **Friday** Mum and Dad are late for work.
"Hurry Mimi, choose a piece of fruit to take to school."

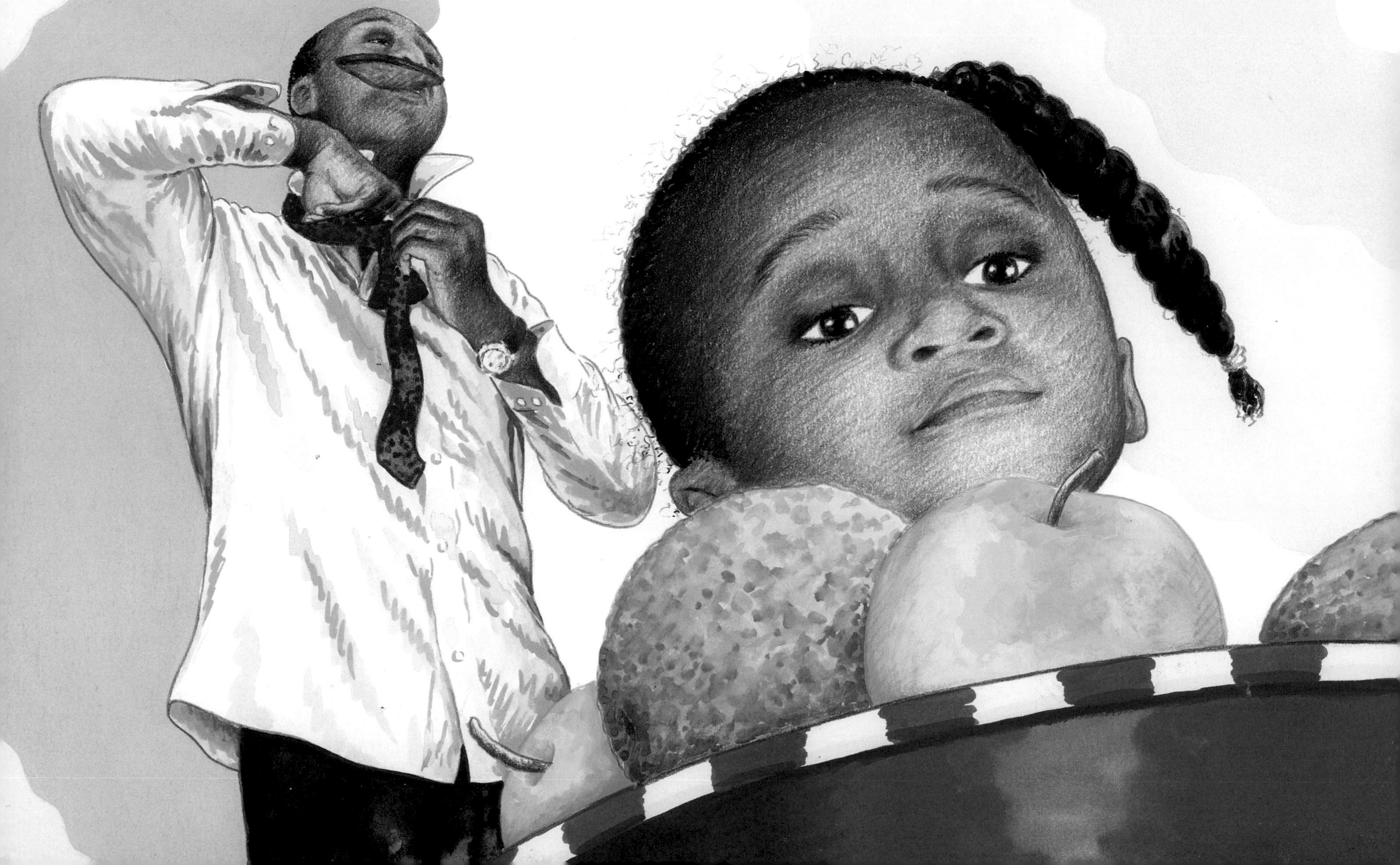

我看着果盘满载的水果，
我应该挑选一个橙子、抑或一个苹果、或者一个梨子呢？
苹果和梨子的颜色和形状令我想起祖母的星期六汤的佛手瓜。

I looked at the bowl full of fruit.
Should I choose an orange, an apple or a pear?
The apple and pear; their colour and shape remind me
of the cho-cho in Grandma's Saturday Soup.

祖母告诉我有关牙买加的水果。
「在牙买加，你可以走路上学，从树上摘一个水果，
一个成熟的芒果，又多汁，又香甜。」

Grandma tells me about the fruits in Jamaica.

"In Jamaica you can walk to school and pick a piece of fruit

from a tree, a ripe mango all juicy and sweet."

放学后，为了奖励我的好成绩，妈妈带我到电影院去。
当我们抵达时，太阳照耀着，但仍然是很寒冷，
我想春天很快便到了。

After school, as a treat for good marks, Mum and Dad took me to the cinema.
When we got there the sun was shining, but it was still cold.
I think springtime is coming.

电影很好看，当我们从电影院出来时，太阳已经开始落下了，
它又大又红，就好像祖母的星期六汤的大南瓜。

The film was great and when we came out the sun was setting over the town.
As it set it was big and orange just like the pumpkin in Grandma's Saturday Soup.

祖母告诉我有关牙买加的日出和日落。
「太阳很早便升起，令你感到清新，为新的一天作好准备。」

Grandma tells me about the sunrise and sunsets in Jamaica.
"The sun rises early and makes you feel good and ready for your day."

「当太阳落下时，月亮便出现，跟着有百万多颗星星像钻石一样在夜空中闪耀。」
百万颗星星，我实在不能想象有这么多的星星。

"When it sets and the moon comes out she is followed by a million stars that look like diamonds twinkling in the night sky."
A million stars, I can't even imagine that many.

星期六早上，我去跳舞班。
音乐很慢和很幽怨。

Saturday morning I went to my dance class. The music was slow and sad.

祖母告诉我有关即兴小调和钢鼓的节奏，有关人们在树荫下玩耍，一株长著像青蕉皮一样的长树叶的奇妙树。
「那音乐令你开心快乐，感到想跟着音乐起舞。」

Grandma tells me about the rhythms of calypso music and steel drums, of people playing under the shade of a tree. A wonderful tree with long leaves that look like the strands of skin from a green banana.
"The music makes you happy and want to dance."

妈妈开车来跳舞班接我。
我们沿着马路驾驶，经过我的学校，在公园转左，途经图书馆，
一直穿越闹市，那里有一间电影院，不会太远了。

Mum picked me up after class. We went by car.
We drove down the road and past my school. We turned left at the park and on past the library. Through the town, there's the cinema and not much further now.

我很饿，实在很饿。我们终于来到祖母家。

I was hungry. Really hungry. At last we arrived at Grandma’s.

我走向大门，已经闻到美味的气味，
是青蕉、佛手瓜、甘薯、汤团、
马铃薯和大南瓜. . .

I ran to the front door and could smell a delicious smell.
It's green bananas, cho-cho and yams, dumplings, potato,
and pumpkin...

青葱、鸡、一大撮祖母的家乡调味料和很多鸡汤。
这就是祖母的星期六汤！

spring onions, chicken, a good pinch of Grandma's
country seasoning and a lot of chicken stock.
It's Grandma's Saturday Soup!

星期日，我们有朋友到家里来吃饭，爸爸和妈妈都是厨艺能手，
但是在这个世界上，祖母的星期六汤是我最喜欢吃的食物。

On **Sunday** we had friends at our house for dinner.
Mum and Dad are good cooks, their food is nice but my favourite food in the whole wide world is **Grandma's Saturday Soup**.